How Spiders Got Eight Legs

Retold by Katherine Mead

Illustrated by Carol O'Malia

STECK-VAUGHN
COMPANY

A Division of Harcourt Brace & Company

www.steck-vaughn.com

Contents

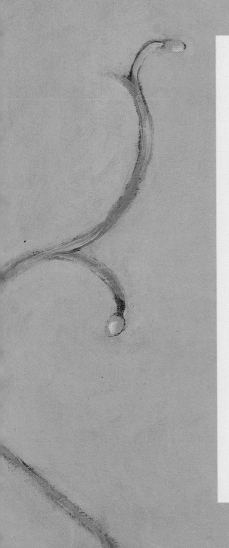

A Big Problem. 3

The Plan. 5

The Promise. 8

Another Promise . . . 14

A Lesson Learned . . 24

A Big Problem

Long ago in Africa, spiders had only two legs. There was one spider who was very selfish. He wanted to be better than all the other animals in the jungle. But he did not like to work hard.

Every year, there was a big race in the jungle. All the animals wanted to win. They practiced running every day. Spider thought, "I am much better than the others. I'll think of a way to win this year's race without working hard."

The Plan

Spider watched all the animals run. He thought that Ostrich, Giraffe, or Cheetah could win the race. Spider could not run as fast as any of them. But he did not worry. He had a plan.

Spider thought, "Ostrich has such strong legs. If I had legs like his, I could win the race." Spider went to the river to see Great Hippo, the hippopotamus. He was the wisest animal. He could grant wishes.

Spider called out, "Great Hippo, I wish to have strong legs like Ostrich."

"Why do you wish to have legs like Ostrich?" Great Hippo asked.

"I have to win the race!" said Spider.

The Promise

Great Hippo said, "I will give you strong legs, but you must promise me something. One day, I will ask you a question. You must answer honestly."

Spider said, "That will be easy." So his wish was granted.

Spider tried to run on his new legs, but it was too hard. He asked Ostrich for help.

Ostrich said, "Watch, my friend. I'll show you how to run with those legs."

Spider watched, but still he could not run.

Spider was mad. He went back to see Great Hippo. He said, "I cannot run with these legs. I wish to have four long legs like Giraffe."

Great Hippo asked, "Why do you wish to have legs like Giraffe?"

Spider said, "I want to take long steps like Giraffe. I have to win the race!"

Great Hippo said, "I will give you four long legs, but you must promise me something. One day, I will ask you a question. You must answer honestly."

Spider said, "That will be easy." So his wish was granted.

Spider tried to run on his long legs, but it was too hard. He asked Giraffe for help.

Giraffe said, "Watch, my friend. I'll show you how to run with those legs."

Spider watched, but still he could not run.

Spider was really mad. He went back to see Great Hippo. He said, "I cannot run on these long legs. I wish for eight legs."

Great Hippo asked, "Why do you wish for eight legs?"

Spider said, "Cheetah is the fastest four-legged animal. I could run twice as fast as Cheetah if I had eight legs."

Another Promise

Great Hippo said, "I will give you eight legs, but you must promise me something. One day, I will ask you a question. You must answer honestly."

Spider said, "That will be easy." So his wish was granted.

Spider tried to run with eight legs, but it was too hard. He asked Cheetah for help.

Cheetah said, "I don't know how to run with eight legs. I could only show you if you had four legs like me."

Spider was madder than ever. He went back to see Great Hippo again. He yelled, "These eight legs don't work! How am I going to win the race?"

Great Hippo did not answer. He just walked into the river to swim.

Spider made his way home. He was still angry. He sat down and thought very hard. How could he win the race with eight legs? Suddenly, he had an idea! He laughed and went to sleep.

On the day of the race, Cheetah could hear someone yelling for help. He said, "That sounds like Spider. I'll go check on him."

Cheetah ran off to Spider's house. Spider was lying down and crying out with pain.

"Spider, what's wrong?" Cheetah asked.

Spider said, "I am very sick. Take me to see Great Hippo. He'll know what to do."

Cheetah said, "Great Hippo is waiting at the finish line. I will take you to him."

Spider climbed on Cheetah's back. Cheetah began to run as fast as he could. The race had already started. Cheetah was behind all the animals. Spider cried louder with pain. Then Cheetah ran faster.

Cheetah ran past the slowest animals. He ran past faster animals. Then Cheetah ran past Ostrich. He ran past Giraffe. Cheetah ran faster and faster until he took the lead.

Spider could see the finish line. He climbed onto the tip of Cheetah's nose. Everyone cheered as Cheetah crossed the finish line. Great Hippo announced, "Cheetah's the winner!"

Spider yelled, "Wait! Cheetah didn't win. I DID! I crossed the finish line first. I won by a nose!"

Great Hippo looked at Spider. He said, "I have a question. Remember that you promised to answer it honestly. Who REALLY won the race?"

A Lesson Learned

Spider was worried. He knew he had to be honest. He said, "I tried to trick all of you. Cheetah is the real winner."

Great Hippo smiled. He said, "Thank you for being honest. Now I will make those eight legs work just right for you."

From then on, spiders everywhere have had eight legs. And they work just right.